SWANS

IN

HALF-

MOURNING

PER SECOND PRESS
P.O. BOX 2704
Iowa City, IA 52244
www.persecondpress.com

Per Second Press books may be purchased for educational, business, or sales promotional use. Please email : persecondpress@gmail.com

Cover design by Bradley Paynter

Third Edition

ISBN 978-0692425152

PER SECOND PRESS

Iowa City, IA

SWANS IN HALF-MOURNING

VI KHI NAO

INTRODUCTION

Swans in Half Mourning, a prose poem in ninety-six parts from Per Second Press, is perhaps the most innovative retelling of a fairy tale that I have ever encountered, one that needs to be experienced, not merely read. Challenging and unconventional, this book is for readers haunted by Hans Christian Andersen's "The Wild Swans," in which a young girl frees her brothers from their enchanted swan form by knitting them coats made of nettles. Vi Khi Nao's version is filled with surprising details: a powerful God who seems curiously human, a bird's experience of desire, an unexpected source of blood found on a conjugal bed.

The heroine, Cynthia, the first in line for the throne, is in love with another princess, Veronika. The passion between the two women, conveyed in beautiful imagery, is irresistible: "Later, Veronika, enervated, will return to the garden of mattresses and allow the horizon of Cynthia's kiss to slip into her mouth." It is this passion, as well as pressure from the antagonist Queen, that will make it hard for Cynthia to keep her six-year vow of silence, one of the conditions to which she must adhere in order to break the spell that hangs over her family.

Her brothers' dilemma demands Cynthia's labor as well as her silence. Like many a fairy-tale heroine, Cynthia's task seems impossible: making six shirts from starwort, which is apparently as painful as nettles. While the brothers wait for their sister to complete her work, we are treated to the many details of a swan's life. The author's attention to the brothers' transformation is speculative fiction at its best. Since they become human for a brief period each day, the brothers are living a dual reality, where the most mundane of human tasks (undressing, using the toilet) can become suddenly impossible. The effect is interesting and sometimes comical, satisfying the modern reader's wish to enter the physical world of the fairy tale. For those who have ever wondered what it is like to slip into animal form, this work proves that it is not only fascinating, but perilous as well. Swans, enchanted or otherwise, should stay away from kitchen work stations.

In the end it is the language itself that is the great triumph of this short work. "The Voice of Veronika spoke: 'I wish sometimes when I come into a room, all of my body parts unassembled like your brothers, Cynthia, so that everyone's speech and the landscape's oration could slowly reassemble me back into poetry and I would become a complete woman.'" Vi Khi Nao does not limit herself to the fairy-tale realm, letting playful mentions of YouTube and Starbucks intrude upon this enchanted

world to leave us in a state of pleasant disorientation. I envy the
reader who is entering this magical place for the first time.

Jan Stinchcomb

I. *size: I like*

All six brothers didn't need wood to incinerate her. Her bones were timber, raw, and human enough to create a pyre. They watched her flame up. The wind whirled her unavoidable flesh devoid of the human spirit into rapture. The tongue of the fire, obsidian and glassy. The brothers couldn't touch her. She couldn't be touched. Her throat was parched from screaming. After all, she was sitting on a wagon in the middle of the road, ready to be carted off into the forest.

II.

Veronika's muscular thighs are falling to pieces. From waiting for her wife too long in the sun. Veronika leans down to collect the fragments of the erotic road, broken into pieces, fragmented. She holds the mirror in her hands to reflect. Her mother-in-law's lips open wide. Veronika gazes down the road of her throat, an impossible place of obliterating, fantastic darkness. The tonsils of her mother-in-law are flickering back and forth like the pages of a book. Home

III.

The King has only one daughter. Her name is Cynthia. His sons: Pok, Ian, Vic, Hoc, Ad, and Eco. But Cynthia is first in line for the throne. *Ha!*

IV.

They got married in the shadow, between a tree and a lake. Cynthia and Veronika's wedding album was made out of 34 ounces of swan's feathers. All six brothers generously contributed their wingspans to their mute little sister. It was a magnificent wedding gift: a powerful symbol of human flight and nuptial clairvoyance. Veronika's love for Cynthia silenced Cynthia, and her silence made the brothers human again.

V.

When Cynthia kissed her, Veronika felt as if she had rolled desire into a ball. For the longest time, when they made love, they had to remain horizontal like a bottle. Inside of Cynthia's mother's glass fortress, everything was transparent. When her mother was hovering over their shoulders, she couldn't convince her lover to moan at a 90-degree angle. She was quick to divert her attention towards the curtain in hopes that it would substitute her sorrow for bliss. The curtain was once a symbol for the parting lips of euphoria.

VI.

After awhile, darkness sank into their lungs and the whole kingdom found itself asleep for eight complete hours.

VII.

For a while, all God did was spin the bottle. The bottle of
darkness. The bottle of light. For a while, life was liquid and
vertiginous.

VIII.

The mother-in-law's scream is extinguished when the King's brother, God, closes the 2.2-centimeter gap between bottle and cork. The bottle will not speak for six years, the duration of Cynthia's silence. Ian once said that when the Queen manipulated the King into giving his daughter's bed sheet to her, those outside of the castle walls stopped breathing.

IX.

Once Pok, second in line for the throne, declared, "Sis, I think your wife's heart wears a spandex miniskirt." If Cynthia could speak, she would have commented, "Yes, as you can see. It can be stretched." Pok places his hand over his mouth. "Sorry, sis, I didn't mean to provoke you into generating sound.'" Later, Veronika, enervated, will return to the garden of mattresses and allow the horizon of Cynthia's kiss to slip into her mouth

X.

The wedding foods were escorted on aluminum wheels. The wedding foods were escorted on aluminum wheels.

XI.

Veronika leaned back into Cynthia's arms as they stood on the edge of the sea. Even the high cliffs were crying and the trees became widowers of the night. Holding Veronika made her feel as if her heart was a green stargazer that had been pressed down by a candle floating in a clear glass of water. Even the brides were wearing matching verdant high heels. Even the glasses were exhaust pipes of desires waiting to be pulled over by the automobile of longing.

XII.

God thinks, yes, shaving armpits will not prevent someone from death.

XIII.

In winter, the curtain swayed, back and forth like the hips of women. Even the Queen's astringent heart knew how to appreciate domestic music during the darkest months of the year. The brothers spent their long days flying over one lake to another. They had to keep their wings active to keep from freezing in midair. Cynthia spent all six winters weaving shirts near the fire. Because the brothers had only fifteen minutes each day to become fleshy and phallic, Veronika went out in the woods, dragging her kimono made out of romantic naturalism: turbulent waterfalls, chalky ostrich-feather. She thumped the ax into the madera block, chopping it into halves. Her wife, Cynthia, desperately waited for her. Veronika had to go deep into the forest to pull wood that had the longest burning time. She knew oak was the best, but the oak trees were 17 kilometers into the forest. 17 kilometers into the forest, there were eucalyptus and walnut, elongated-burning-time trees. Veronika's kimono wouldn't let her go very far and she wasn't willing to drop the dress for mere bucolic formality.

XIV.

Everyone knew that the Queen was a slow-walking eucalyptus.

XV.

When the King walked his daughter down the aisle, his future daughter-in-law's smile was radiating so brightly that it made his heart hurt. His heart felt like an archaic well, dripping water and sound. Hand placed on his arm, his daughter appeared to him like a savage beauty, stringing stalks of white asparagus along the back of her hem. She was decorated in an oyster wedding dress made out of ivory silk organza, chiffon, and georgette. Personally designed by Alexander McQueen for the connubial occasion. The Queen, his wife, loved the dress so fervently that she nearly fustigated her daughter's eyes out in her attempt to steal the dress from her. With the camera rolling, the King intervened. He shouted, "Darling Witch, you had your wedding already. Drop the dress. This is your daughter's breath. This is her day." The Queen turned to the King, "But my sweet husband—." The King interrupted, "This is her wedding. Stop being so selfish! Drop the dress!" The Queen fumed at the King and turned to a pre-suicidal Alexander McQueen, stating *sotto voce*, "Mark my words, Lord of Tailoring, the King will pay for this! For humiliating me in front of YouTube."

XVI.

The queen's revenge: biweekly, though not bisexually, the mother-in-law sought Cynthia out to make her laugh. The Queen was neither a clown nor a comedian. Her first joke, "......insert bad joke." Nonetheless, Veronika and the brothers rushed to her comedic table to reinforce neutrality and sadness. To force, potentially, an echo to recede back into its sonic cave, Eco and Ad plucked their plumage and piled it on Cynthia's lips as a means to suppress Cynthia's risible throat. As long as she didn't laugh, they would have a chance.

XVII.

When they couldn't wait any longer, a note, scribbled urgently, stitched with starwort to the hem of the curtain: "Make love to me, Veronika."

XVIII.

At first, God plans on cutting the horizon into smaller pieces and stripes by converting electrical wires into scissors and stuffing the horizon into the bottle. God learns that blowing is the fastest route of transformation and the quickest way of getting tedious, evolutionary chores done. Whenever he wishes to destitute or dilute a piece of land, he blows the sea and the wind violently. It would take too long to erase one acre of landscape at a time. He remembered this when he blew Adam into life. He realized that it would probably have taken him forever if he had used a surgical blade and outlined Adam's body on a wet slat of dirt, one front and one back, and outlined Adam's shadow and stuffed it into the clay to create his soul. The Queen knew the cruelty of slowness, of stitching, of the inability to find humor in a task.

XIX.

At the beginning of their courtship, the eyes of all birds remained closed.

XX.

Even the shadow had to watch its footsteps before the Queen.
Everyone watched their footsteps before the Queen. Their eyes,
their own security camera.

XXI.

How possible is it to have an orgasm without making a sound?

Not, very

XXII.

At night, when the light collapsed onto pillowcases, the loneliness of the night made the brothers feel as if they had lived 5% of their life in light and the other 95% in shadow. Cynthia got out of bed, walked to the basin near the night table, and scooped out a handful of birdseed. She leaned out of the window and pressed her overworked and over-occupied hand out into the naked, nocturnal air. Cued by the habitual music of her gesture, her brothers flocked towards her. Their wings beat rapidly and they pecked until her hand became concave like a crater. Usually, written on her fingers and palm: "Good evening, Ian, Pok, Ad, Hoc, Vic, Eco. Tell me what the air is like five miles from here." Tonight her hand has been scrubbed clean with olive oil and lime and de-graffitized.

XXIII.

God stylizes his hair short and blond by going down on the sun.

XXIV.

The King and Hoc, who wished to accompany his father on a business trip, took a train ride to the edge of New York before flying to Iceland. During the diplomatic trip, the King and Hoc thrust their faces forward into the air, gelid, trapped by the darkness of the Icelandic landscape, to greet their new agricultural rivals. The King remembered, yes, they had built so many outdoor shower stalls on their own agrarian fields for pastoral citizens' washing. Hoc became a man, naked and iced, during the business transaction. When they came back from their trip, Veronika had no choice but to ask the King what happened between the two of them. The King leaned back and smiled. He thought, yes, they were convinced.

XXV.

God is thinking about plugging the Queen's vocal cords with the cork. God is indecisive. God's indecision is largely due to his pleasure. Should he end it now and begin with something else or should he continue to import a person's pain, trap it in a bottle, and use its sonic dementia to generate the next human twilight?

XXVI.

"Cynthia, I think I have fallen in love with her," declared Hoc in his human mouth.

XXVII.

On her knees at the edge of the bathtub, Veronika rubbed thyme unguent on her beloved's hand. To prevent carpal tunnel syndrome from birthing as a result of the endless stitching, Veronika massaged her hands every day for an hour. Veronika could feel Cynthia's blood thickening and heating from the kneading. When finished, Veronika pressed her mouth near the King's daughter's ear: "Cynthia, I know it has only been three months, I've missed your voice dearly. I can't wait for the day when the white ribbons of your voice unravel into my ear." ℘

XXVIII.

The Queen glanced at her daughter and laughed deeply into the throat of the main foyer.

XXIX.

In the third year of unwinding the spell, Cynthia's hands began to bleed. The cuticles became corrugated, translucent eyes that cried red tears. All the tips of Cynthia's fingers, including the pinky, had become abraded from the perpetual floral threading. When Cynthia entered her, Veronika felt as if she were sanding, waxing, and shining her clitoris like a pair of old shoes. The blood dripped and plopped, like rain, into aluminum buckets near Cynthia and Veronika's conjugal bed. Getting out of bed to grab hand towels, Veronika asked, "Darling, are you alright?"

XXX.

At the dinner table, two types of wine were served: one red, one white. Red wine: Cynthia's blood. White wine: her tears.

XXXI.

Early in their courtship, Veronika would walk Cynthia along the lake, hand in hand, watching the swans' beaks drink in the beacon of water laminated by the falling light. Cynthia's hair would fall over her shoulder like six mute pieces of tupperware falling off the edge of a table.

XXXII.

"Sister, are you done yet?" the brother cried. 1) When Cynthia tossed the shirts into the air and when the shirts climbed onto the brothers' bodies, the forest began to open its arboreal thighs to the sky.

XXXIII.

For several years after their wedding night, Cynthia and Veronika remained abstinent. They didn't climb each other's bodies because they were afraid of making a sound. Of converting their mythological flesh into desire, and desire into music.

XXXIV.

Borrowing God's memory, Cynthia wished she could easily blow the floral fabric of starwort into six shirts.

XXXV.

The Voice of Veronika spoke: "I wish sometimes when I come into a room, all of my body parts would disassemble like your brothers, Cynthia, so that everyone's speech and the landscape's oration could slowly reassemble me back into poetry and I would become a complete woman."

XXXVI.

"Sister, are the shirts ready yet?" the brothers asked in between panels of light. When Veronika pinned her to the bed, Cynthia was able to understand the expansion of her brothers' wings.

XXXVII.

The Queen arched her back, stretched her hands towards the sky, and yawned.

XXXVIII.

Cynthia had stashed their finished shirts in a closet. There were five hanging there. She was working on the last shirt. They felt hope climb their throats like a croaking frog.

XXXIX.

God is ~~on his knees,~~ his monarchal butt cheeks pointing [exposed] at the
empyrean theater of human existence. There. There. Yes, it's
true he has lowered the protean skin [uncut] of the sky and shepherded
it into a definite vessel. And, yes, it means he has already blown
the horizon into the neck of a recumbent bottle. The landscape
of the mother-in-law's memory can be asphyxiated, then
preserved. He holds the cork of the bottle 2.2 centimeters away
from the mouth of the bottle.

XL.

The King gazed at the cornfield and confidently talked to himself, "The corn had been bloated. It was a bad year for the corn."

XLI.

Sitting on a bench in the park, the sunlight folded Veronika's body into Cynthia's. They united as one diurnal envelope of feminine ontology into one fold. However, Veronika's thighs were falling to pieces, as if they were made of glass, shattering on the surface of the ground.

XLII.

The bleeding continued every night for the next four years. Veronika took Cynthia into her arms and encouraged her to cry into the pocket of her lingerie. In the morning, Veronika's body was dressed in a diffusion of gore, as if Veronika had crushed an entire population of convergent ladybugs.

XLIII.

Veronika was sliding her fingertips, teaching her to bend back the bow. Cynthia's eyelashes dropped lower and lower like servants of light, black angels closing the gap between the electrical wire of Veronika's shoulder and the sky of Cynthia's hand as she brushed her hair behind her back. Veronika turned her head. The symmetry of their gaze bound the heart of the bow to the arrow as Cynthia's fingers overlapped Veronika's. In union, they pulled back the taut string and the arrow plunged.

XLIV.

The servants worked day and night in preparation for the wedding. The reception set the world record for largest wedding party ever.

XLV.

From behind, Veronika, "Darling, tell me what you are thinking. Without telling me what it is that you are thinking."

XLVI.

The fifth year into Cynthia's voice in full mourning, the King turned to his beloved Cynthia, "My daughter, as soon as you regain your voice, I am turning the kingdom over to you. You will become Queen Cynthia."

XLVII.

The Queen, afraid of losing her station and position in society, began to engage in full, tactless warfare with a reticent Cynthia. The brothers, armored in full regalia, plunged into their nightly guarding shifts. The brothers were afraid to make their flight across the lake. Night and day, with Veronika, they trafficked Cynthia's bed quarters as she sewed continuously, 20 hours a day, sleeping only four hours. Excessively over-caffeinated, Cynthia didn't want to ever gaze at another Starbucks coffee mug for the rest of her life.

XLVIII.

The sea was drifting by the land of featherlike vanes fastened to the shaft of pleasure. Is this the displeasure?

XLIX.

The Queen shaved her armpits over a copper basin.

L.

News of Uncle Antonioni's aggressive proposition towards his future daughter-in-law reached the King. In the middle of his hippopotamus and squirrel hunt, the King had Antonioni extracted from his camping ground, anesthetized by his own personal surgeon, and had a Tahitian artist flown in to tattoo his forehead with "NO!"; his right cheek, "cannot"; his left cheek, "have"; and below his lips and above the apex of his lower jaw, "her" in Bauhaus 93 font. Up-close, the "NO" on his corrugated skin made his forehead look like the entrance of a dingy bar. After the invasion of black pigment, the septuagenarian uncle stopped asking.

LI.

God gets up from the comfort of lying down, ties shoelaces made of angel hair, and shoves the bottle into a hay bale.

LII.

Veronika was sitting on the bench, constructing a birdhouse made out of king-size pillowcases, bed sheets, plexiglass, and wood. When the construction was complete, the two pillowcases appeared as if they had been blown into angulated balloons giving each other mouth-to-mouth resuscitation. The brothers trotted one by one into their shelter through the plexiglass hole tucked beneath the bottom end of the bed sheets. Above them the plexiglassed skylight. When they fell asleep, the light emanating from outside stroked the fragility of their throbbing plumage. It appeared as if six white hearts were quivering in a diminutive white tent, waiting for the eyes of the X-Acto knives to impale their lungs. White on white. Milk and desire at their height of pleasure. Sleep was pleasure. Opening their eyes was even more pleasurable. Veronika observed, "When they are sleeping, their eyelids look like crescent moons that have fallen into a bowl of milk."

LIII.

God gets up from the comfort of lying down, ties shoelaces made of angel hair, and shoves the bottle into a hay bale.

LIV.

The Voice of Eco speaks: "We must tell you, sis and Veronika, what we did to the Queen yesterday, the day that we were unable to see you. We pulled a prank we had planned for weeks. It happened on one of those days when the air was thick and the humidity made everyone's body lament. The Queen was taking her afternoon nap when we flew into her sleeping chamber. We flew in five minutes before our transformation of euphoria. When she cracked open her eyes ten minutes into our deplaned, naked state, she was mopping her eyes back and forth with the back of her hand, flummoxed by the appearance before her. I guess she hadn't been exposed to so many upside-down coke bottles all at once! Especially from all six of her sons. "Hello, Mother," we all greeted in unison. We couldn't tell from her expression if she wanted to fuck us or whack us. Five minutes later, she was chasing and clouting our plumage with a flywhisk until we flew out of her window."

LV.

God erases the sun with a white eraser and dresses the sun's face in charcoal. Veronika is on the edge. Making—

1) Cynthia is standing there near the closet
2) And Veronika watches her unveil her skin from a blouse
3) She is facing the closet
4) She watches her, not completely naked in the light
5) Not completely naked for nakedness' sake
6) Without her there, the darkness stops breathing
7) She watches her without relinquishing
8) Cynthia's bra straps appear to her like window frames on a   train
9) She gazes into her back
10) She sees a moving, invisible landscape of oxygen and ephemeral ribs
11) Insulated by skin
12) Veronika lingers her fingers delicately
13) The oxygen tank beneath Cynthia's skin
14) Blows her heart backwards into Veronika's breasts
15) The wind is tossing the heads of daffodils
16) As she falls back and Veronika holds her
17) Her arms around her waist
18) She is a piece of solid earth
19) Meeting the confluence of rivers of her arms

20) As the soft conifers residing on the valley of her chest
21) Separate her breath from her breath
22) Her sash from her sash
23) Veronika unstraps the window frames and slides them off her
24) She is she
25) A landscape liberated from the constraints of architecture
26) A windowsill is a windowsill
27) Veronika removes the window, this landscape off her
28) It falls, unhinged, onto the floorboard
29) She tosses the landscape in the air
30) The architecture outside of Cynthia descends
31) When she gazes out of the window of her house
32) The sky is one shoulder turning its empyrean contours
33) The cloud
34) The sky
35) The desire
36) As Cynthia leans into the closet space of ardor
37) Her knees grow weak from holding up the sky
38) And when she bends, as light sometimes bends
39) Or she spreads as sometimes light spreads
40) Her hair gathers like grass across the invisible bra line
41) As her face sinks into Cynthia's hair
42) As sometimes dew and fog take turns blowing the night into the mouth of sensuality

43) And Veronika whispers into her ear, "When will the boat of your tongue drift into the sea of my mouth?"

LVI.

Six swans floated near the rim of the well, attempting to vibrate their sonic breath into the dark throat of the earth.

LVII.

The King's diplomats gathered around the table. Veronika had walked into the palace, escorted by twenty servants dressed like quail eggs, and was followed by her mother, Queen Mungbean, and her father, King Awesome. The Awesome Empire resided just short of 3,000 kilometers away from Princess Cynthia and her father, King Monocle. Seating arrangements were made several months in advance. The space between Veronika's chair and Cynthia's was 2 millimeters. During the grand banquet, saturated with a cacophony of voices in celebration of the successful breeding of goats between two kingdoms, Cynthia turned to Veronika and asked, "I haven't plucked my eyebrows lately, but would you like to go on a date with me?"

LVIII.

Sitting next to the marvelous Veronika, Cynthia's shoulder
blushed.

LIX.

In the middle of the prairie, Uncle Antonioni turned to Cynthia

1) "Your fiancé, Veronika. WOW! She is a beauty!"
2) Cynthia smiled.

> "I know you cannot speak, but a nod of the head will do. I can beseech the Queen, on your behalf, of course, on your behalf, to have the spell reversed or shortened, say instead of six years, five and three quarters. Under the condition that you annul the wedding and allow me to take Veronika as my wife." Cynthia took out a Sharpie tucked above her ear and wrote on his arm, "NO! You cannot have her."

5 3/4

LX.

"Beloved sister, we are anxious to be human again. We don't mean to rush you. You have no idea how much we appreciate having a tailbone at a consistent height of three feet above the ground instead of having its inconsistency, a fluctuation of one centimeter at times and other times 32,780 feet above the Ivory Coast of West Africa, obscuring our shit-making process. We have tried to avoid the heads of the court, but our understanding of gravity remains concealed to us at such height."

LXI.

They nearly plunged one of the Princes, Prince Hoc to be precise, in boiling water. He had gotten so close to the chef's table as he prepared the wedding platters, pecking on the luminous, glittering roe. Fortunately, he turned into a man seated at the end of the end of the table and saved his own life before the edge of the chef's butcher knife cut into his neck. The chef had him squeezed by the neck, until suddenly his neck expanded to the circumference of an electrical post. The chef had no choice but to release him.

LXII.

Veronika's heart sits on the ethereal chair of her chest, waiting for Cynthia.

LXIII.

Cynthia and Veronika were sitting close like ingredients. One canister of flour sitting next to a canister of sugar. As their feminine forms exchanged translucent powder. With one another. Pre-suffocation. Not cupcake, but pre-cupcake.

LXIV.

Cynthia nearly choked on the marshmallow trying to hold back her laughter.

LXV.

God lies on his belly counting the stars.

LXVI.

Hoc confessed to Cynthia, "I am so confused, Cynth. Sometimes I think I possess human desires, the desire to fuck a woman, and at other times not. More often now, closer to the latter. But perhaps being a bird has enfeebled any virulent drives in me. I have begun to have avian impulses. I have fallen for a ruby-throated hummingbird whose heart beats faster than most. She called herself by the name of Spur. She does everything in the spur of a moment. Have you seen her iridescent plumage? Have you experienced her rapid vibration? You know Spur flies backwards and I am so dazzled at what she can do. And then there is the problem of size. I used to fall for women who overpower me. You remembered Mica Storm, the STORM? Yeah, her. Being next to Spur, I feel as if she were David and I, Goliath. Sometimes I think my passion could squash her like a pancake. When I was a full-time man, all I wanted to do was masturbate and fuck. After all, I was fucking fourteen. And now, and now, all I want to do is dig my face in grass and drop worms into Spur's throat. Of course, I chew it into bite sizes so she doesn't choke. I would try to find worms with six or eight hearts or earthworms with twenty-seven stomachs or something that ridiculous and feed them to her. Just so that its nutrition would properly regulate her body temperature and she would fly better and be healthier. I think I need to see a therapist."

LXVII.

Six naked men bent over the well, arms linked. Their heliotropic butt cheeks mooned the afternoon star.

LXVIII.

The wedding platters were arranged meticulously before being escorted out on aluminum wheels. The first dish that was ushered out: Swan In Half-Mourning, followed by Rootless Baguette:

1) d. 1/ SWAN DEMI-DEUIL: The chef had 7-ounces of black truffle juice. Beneath the chin, the fat around the ankle sagged. The truffle juice got underneath the skin and overnight the swan sat in the obsidian darkness drinking in the truffle with the floppy mouth created by the skin fat.

2) d. 2/ ROOTLESS BAGUETTE: It appeared that it was too short and it appeared as if it couldn't hold air or stem. The rootless baguette stood before the mouths of the wedding guests, an apotheosis, lost in the subconscious space of a grape. Before dangling in space, it had been dipped in plastic, molded from the ruin of flour, into a crispy consciousness of carbohydrate and butter. The thing was a little Napoleon, its first sexual encounter with a seedless stem. Six stainless steel poles lift the baquette from its burrow. Before this, it was deplaned from a hydraulic pool of peanut oil.

Sixty thousand, two hundred, and three wedding guests hijacked these appetizers into the memories made by their mouths.

60, 203

LXIX.

All six brothers got on their knees and for fifteen minute of their humanity said, "Sis, come here, we want to each take turns and wash your hands and feet." The brothers genuflected and with a hand towel tossed over their shoulders and thick towels spread on their knees, they uttered: "Princess Cynthia, our Queen to be, this is a symbol of our infinite gratitude for sewing us back into existence. May the fresh water carried from the mountain un-coarse your hands and freshen your footsteps so that you may have the courage to nurture our father's kingdom back to health." Cynthia's slender legs were dipped into a wooden bucket.

LXX.

Veronika wouldn't let the servants chop wood. She wanted to split the earth in halves by herself.

LXXI.

The brothers' human appearance occurred once a day at exactly three in the afternoon. As soon as the brothers turned into their human forms, there was intense merriment in the kingdom. The brothers airlifted Cynthia around the court. Veronika joined, fox-trotting along with them. They hip-hopped their hips around the pillars of the royal rooms. To prevent Cynthia from laughing with delight and joy, they stuffed her mouth with marshmallows. Once the King teased, "You all have stuffed my little Princess with a baby pillow. Is she going to inhale all your dreams and leave all your memory abandoned in a sugar canister?" Chef Grant Achatz personally designed the square pillows, 2cm by 2 cm, 4 square pillows lay one head, by freezing beer froth and sea foam, dehydrating and whitening the edge of the Belgian endives inside the deflateable pillows with cream so that when the pillows melted, the heads of the brothers were sonically awake to the crunchy air of these curly-leaved endives. From a distance, when these Achatz pillows were arranged on white Flora Danica platters, the brothers' bedding, the whole thing looked like a slow-moving, iced, diminutive plateau of opulent glacier. The heads of the brothers sink in.

LXXII.

In the evening, after washing her wife's face, Veronika massaged Cynthia's eyes with a thin coat of shea butter. She orbited her fingertips on the left eye and the right eye fifty times. The darkness had strained her eyes as she sewed. As she sewed.

LXXIII.

On the days it rained, Veronika leaned against the pillar holding up a large black umbrella. The six swans flew underneath and waited for the storm to pass. Their webbed feet paced back and forth inside the radius of the umbrella. Their feet were sleek, as if they had been polished by a shoemaker.

LXXIV.

Time is sitting on the corner, in a chair, perhaps, feeling dust
and light collecting a speckleless shadow. And then there's the
armor of the living, which no one has a decent say on how it
should sit.

LXXV.

The King turned to Ad, "Does the summer feel fat to you, son?"
Ad replied, "No, Father, hardly at all."

LXXVI.

The brothers liked to fasten their footsteps to the sea before landing. This was to say: feet do not need seatbelts to latch as long as their feet are surrounded by the nostalgia of persistent return.

LXXVII.

Some days, the brothers ran their hands through the shirts their sister had sewn for them. Patiently awaiting their human form. As if the shirts had kidnapped their bodies instead of the Queen. Their sister had worked hard. She worked hard. One shirt a year. Three years hung inside the closet. Three years. Three shirts.

LXXVIII.

To break the spell, Cynthia's task: knitting six shirts, one shirt for each brother.

LXXIX.

In winter, for Cynthia, making love to Veronika was like turning a pillowcase inside out. Her breath spread like snow on her body. Even the barren landscape was aching.

LXXX.

God is sweeping the landscape, lying horizontally on the glassy bed closer to the bottom end of the bottle. It seems as if the landscape is trying to climb up the asphyxiated air, verdant back lying on verdant back.

LXXXI.

All six brothers folded their white shirts neatly into drawers. Fifteen minutes each day as humans – folding their 15-minute-white shirts and 15-minute-white pants into laundry baskets. They liked to get naked before the reality of their transformation snatched them away.

LXXXII.

Cynthia had been trained as a vocalist.

is this
enough

for 1 section?
for 1 whole

page?

I dunno.

LXXXIII.

Sometimes Hoc flew towards the crater of light. As falling in love had made him radiate. Even as a waterbird, flying was a way of using air to snorkel. The monogamous brothers had no choice but to follow in tow. When they flew towards the sun, their anti-subarctic hearts became sultry with heat.

LXXXIV.

At the banquet: the way she was looking at Veronika, it seemed as if she were tilting the room. More to the left. More to the left. The room wasn't going to spill over like a glass of milk. The door had been standing ajar, like a man with his legs spread an inch apart.

LXXXV.

Ian sat on the electrical wire stapled to two flying buttresses of the cathedral. He was trying to see how long he could keep his eyes open without blinking.

LXXXVI.

Cynthia's back was bent over the light, cutting the thread stitched to the starwort flesh while Veronika baked thirteen loaves of traditional Jordanian bread so that the brothers did not have to dig their bills in trash bins in search of leavened edibles. The gap between their bills hollered: *Shrak, shrak, shrak, shrak.*

LXXXVII.

The brothers woke up from their avian dreams. They dreamt
that their avian forms were baptized by the shirts.

LXXXVIII.

Lucifer, God's brother, doesn't know better. He finds the bottle tucked into the spiral wall of a hay bale, removes it, fumbling with it before uncorking it. His curiosity gets the better of him; he drinks its contents down with one gulp. The Queen's voice rattles inside his esophagus. Some people believe this was how the snake got its rattle, from the Devil choking on the Queen's voice.

LXXXIX.

The birds waddled over to a bowl of wine and broken piles of bread sitting in a basket.

XC.

The King watched the cows' moos drag their thighs along the alfalfa field. The King murmured something softly to the ground. The dragonflies hovering on the lips of the tulips could hear the vibration.

XCI.

The brothers ushered her soul forward. What more to do? What more to do than to fulfill that last finite gesture: tossing the shirts over the ascending swans. The light withdrew darkness into its bosom and the brothers were human again.

XCII.

Under the tutelage of Alexander McQueen, Cynthia was able to create mesmerizing savage patterns for the shirts. Cynthia had to inject life-preservatives into the shirts to keep them young, fresh, and mortal-less. She realized this lesson six days into sewing the collar of one shirt. The shirt shrank into a white grape. Two weeks into the stitching, the shirt became a white raisin.

XCIII.

Veronika sipped a cup of genmaicha green tea and one eyelash
fell into the cup.

XCIV.

The brothers were waddling back and forth on the 88th floor of the palace waiting in line to use the toilet. Typically, they each had their own toilet to themselves, but the butler who took them up to the one-bathroom penthouse for a pre-elimination view left the swan brothers to tend to their own defecatory services. Eco sighed, "Ah," as his human butt cheeks kissed the rim of the toilet seat. The other brothers urged him to hurry up. Eco had taken way too long to release. They wondered what he had eaten. Eco suggested, "Why don't you take the elevator and find yourself a floor to poop on. I am busy here." The other brothers didn't really want to take that path. They hadn't timed how long was left of their 15 human minutes and they didn't want to be trapped on some random floor where the butler couldn't find them. Eco took too long and in the midst of finishing off, he found himself transformed, sitting pulvinatedly on the toilet sea as if the toilet had hatched out a swan. Indeed it did. The human hand that held on to a crumpled up toilet paper evaporated into the air. The toilet paper, ownerless, had no choice but to flutter onto the ceramic bathroom tile, descending slowly like a feather. Eco flapped his wing back and forth. Handless, he attempted to handle the flusher, but without the proper weight distribution or pressure the flusher wouldn't budge. After several attempts, an idea rattled his imagination. He took one deep breath and ascended the air until one of his wedded feet pressed onto the flusher. He rocked back and forth on it before plummeting all his weight on it. He fell down and twirled several times before he heard the water swishing down. He wished one of the brothers were in there with him to see what he had accomplished. He walked out of the bathroom to find his brothers waddling and wandering aimlessly before a glass window the size of a tennis court.

XCV.

The first words that fluttered weakly out of Cynthia's lips, "Yes, I do."

XCVI.

Aviary shirts flew on the shoulders of the brothers. Birds on birds. They crossed the gentle prairie.

VI KHI NAO was born in Long Khanh, Vietnam, in 1979. In 2013, she graduated with an MFA in fiction from Brown University, where she received the John Hawkes and Feldman Prizes in fiction and the Kim Ann Arkstark Memorial Awards in poetry. Vi's work includes poetry, fiction, film and cross-genre collaboration. She is the author of two novellas, *Swans In Half-Mourning* (2013) and *The Vanishing Point of Desire* (2011), and was the winner of 2015 Nightboat Poetry Prize.

45762670R00070

Made in the USA
Charleston, SC
01 September 2015